The Birth-Order Blues

BY JOAN DRESCHER

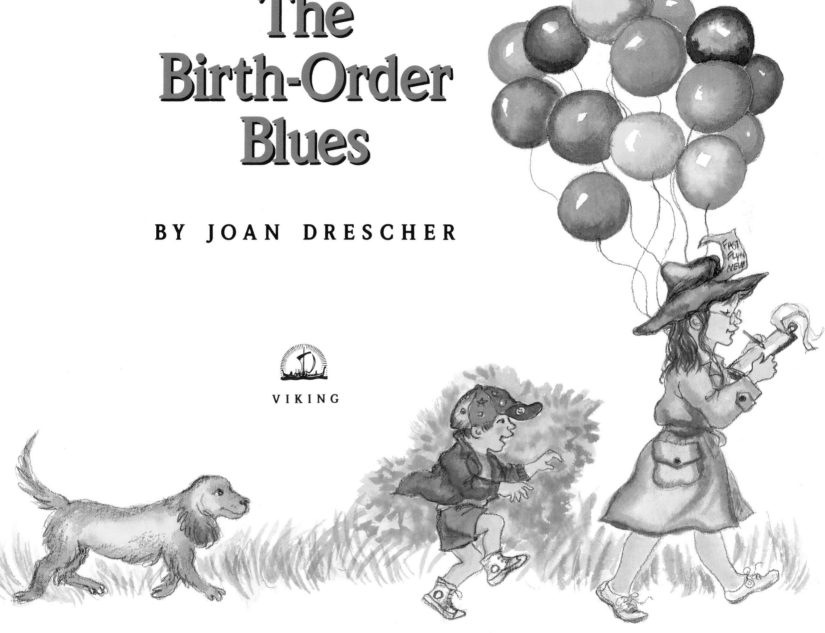

VIKING

Thanks to the many elementary-school children
throughout New England who shared their feelings about
their places in their families and who were part of
the Birth-Order Blues survey.

VIKING
Published by the Penguin Group
Penguin Books USA Inc., 375 Hudson Street, New York, New York 10014, U.S.A.
Penguin Books Ltd, 27 Wrights Lane, London W8 5TZ, England
Penguin Books Australia Ltd, Ringwood, Victoria, Australia
Penguin Books Canada Ltd, 10 Alcorn Avenue, Toronto, Ontario, Canada M4V 3B2
Penguin Books (N.Z.) Ltd, 182–190 Wairau Road, Auckland 10, New Zealand

Penguin Books Ltd, Registered Offices: Harmondsworth, Middlesex, England

First published in 1993 by Viking, a division of Penguin Books USA Inc.

1   3   5   7   9   10   8   6   4   2

Library of Congress Cataloging-in-Publication Data
Drescher, Joan E. Birth order blues / written and illustrated by Joan Drescher.   p.   cm.
Summary: A school newspaper reporter surveys kids on how they feel about
being born first, last, or in the middle of their family's hierarchy.
I S B N   0 - 6 7 0 - 8 3 6 2 1 - 4
[1. Birth order—Fiction.   2. Family—Fiction.]   I. Title.
PZ7.D78384Bi   1993   [E]—dc20   92-41928   CIP   AC

To my children, Lisa, Kimberly, and Ken
—oldest, middle, and youngest—
and to my younger sister Jean
who all inspired me to create this book.

Hi! I'm Millicent Brown, and I'm a reporter for *The Fast Flyer News*. For my next article I'm going to take a survey about something. Hmmm. . . . What topic can I ask questions about?

Wait a second—is that little creep Sam following me around *again*? Sometimes I wish I had an *older* brother instead of a younger one.

All the kids I know complain about their places in the family. Everyone thinks the other guys have the best deal. So I'm going to call my survey the Birth-Order Blues!

Now, let's see . . . who should I use for my survey? Here we go—some friends from school:

Fred

Millicent

Sam

OLDEST

Kim

MIDDLE

Beth
(between Tim and Terry)

YOUNGEST

Rollin' Ralph

Kim's sisters and brothers
Su, May, Jon, and Lee

ONLY CHILD

Tony

Ralph's brother and sisters
Kenny, Molly, and Mary

7

9

11

My big brother always gets to one car window first, and my little brother cries when he can't see. So who gets squashed in the middle? You guessed it.

13

. . . and sometimes I'm the big sister.

Kenny
at 6 months

Kenny with Mom
and Dad

Kenny
takes a nap

Molly
and her dolly

Molly's
first ride

Mary's
first bite

ROLLIN' RALPH

I have one older brother and two older sisters, and my parents were sick of taking pictures by the time I was born. I didn't even get recorded in a baby book! I guess everything I do is a rerun.

17

When you're the youngest, you get everyone's old toys and clothes and the older kids boss you around like crazy! And you're lucky if there's any space left on the refrigerator door for your pictures.

18

19

My pictures get the whole refrigerator door, and I'm the only kid opening presents on Christmas in our house. Sometimes that's nice, and sometimes it's lonely.

Thank you, Tony! Thank you, everyone! Now, let's get down to business. Peter needs to take a picture for *The Fast Flyer News*, our newspaper, to go with the survey.

I want to show my four subjects—that's Kim, Beth, Ralph, and Tony—and all their brothers and sisters, too. Let's have the littlest in the front, the tallest in the back, and the in-betweens in the middle.

24

25

Listen, everybody! It doesn't matter if you're born first, last, in the middle, or only; there is no one quite like you! That's why each of you gets a balloon of a different color for being in my survey. Everyone is different (and special!) and that's what makes families work.

28

The Fast Flyer News

FREE

Printed by Central Elementary School

MILLICENT'S MAGNIFICENT BIRTH-ORDER BLUES SURVEY

by Millicent Brown
Chief Reporter

In a recent survey entitled the Birth-Order Blues, four kids from Central Elementary were interviewed about their places in their families. Kim (oldest), Beth (middle), Ralph (youngest), and Tony (only) each had complaints and thought the others had the best deal. However, everyone realized that no matter where you fit into your family, there are good things about being the oldest, middle, youngest, or only kid.

The final conclusion is that every child in a family is important in making the whole family what it is, and that we're all unique and special.

To celebrate their differences, each child in the survey was given a balloon of a different color. Congratulations, everyone, on a magnificent Birth-Order Rainbow!

31

Hey! Here is Millicent's Birth-Order Blues survey! Now you can try it out on your friends.

Wait a minute, kid, who do you think you are? Taking my hat, my clipboard, and my idea? Typical!

BIRTH-ORDER BLUES SURVEY

Where do you fit into your family?   Oldest   Middle   Youngest   Only

What are the best things about your place in the family?
What are the worst things? How do you feel about your place in the family?

OTHER STUFF TO DO

Take a count. How many kids in your class or group are:
Oldest   Middle   Youngest   Only

Write about how it would feel to change places with someone in your family (it could even be your dog!). What would your day be like? Draw a picture of you and your family.